Electronic Pet Care

by Tracey West

featuring
CyberGirl

SCHOLASTIC INC.

New York   Toronto   London   Auckland   Sydney

The author wishes to thank
The Dragon and the Unicorn bookstore
of Sparkill, New York,
for help with electronic research.

ISBN 0-590-18919-0

12 11 10 9 8 7 6   7 8 9/9 0 1 2/0

Cover and interior illustrations
and book design by Joan Ferrigno

Printed in the U.S.A.   14

First Scholastic printing, July 1997

Hi! I'm CyberGirl. I live in cyberspace. What? You've never heard of cyberspace? I bet you've been there before. It's the world inside all computers.

My world is a lot like yours. I go to school. I hang out with my friends. I even have pets.

Now the pets of my world have come to your world. Millions of them are living on Earth now. They live inside devices that hang on keychains. The people of your world call them lots of different names: electronic pets, interactive pets, virtual pets, cybertoys, and more!

Electronic pets need lots of love, care, and attention, just like real pets. They need you to feed them when they're hungry, and take them to the doctor when they get sick. They need you to play with them, give them treats, and turn out the lights when it's time to sleep. They even need you to clean up after them when they go to the bathroom!

Taking care of an electronic pet can be a lot of fun, but it's not always easy. That's why I traveled millions of light-years to come to your planet. I've been taking care of electronic pets for a long time, and I thought you might need a helping hand.

In this book, you'll find lots of tips for keeping your electronic pet healthy and happy. I'll also tell you some fun ways to wear your pet, share your pet, throw a party for your pet, and play with your pet.

Best of all, there's a special Pet Diary at the back of this book so that you can keep track of your pet every day. There's room to keep track of three different pets!

When you're done with this book, I'll zip back home to cyberspace. But don't worry. You'll still have your electronic pet to keep you company!

CHAPTER ONE
It Began in Japan

Beep beep beep.

In November 1996, the sound of thousands of electronic pets hatching could be heard all over cities in Japan. Bandai's TAMAGOTCHI™ was the first electronic pet to travel from cyberspace to Earth. People in Japan quickly fell in love with the little bird-creature, which lived inside a colorful plastic egg.

TAMAGOTCHI was an instant hit. In three months, over three million of the pets were sold. As soon as the pets reached toy stores, they sold out. In Tokyo, two thousand people camped out one night to wait for a store to open.

It isn't just kids in Japan who are crazy for TAMAGOTCHI. Adults love their electronic pets, too. Why did these pets start such a big craze?

One reason is that Japan is a crowded country. Many people live in small apartments and don't have room for real pets. Electronic pets are the perfect solution. They are small enough to fit in a pocket.

Many people like taking care of their electronic pets because it's a game. They have fun trying to get a high score and making their pets last a long, long time.

Others use their electronic pets to make a fashion statement. They collect the different colors and styles.

A few months after TAMAGOTCHI hit Japan, the pets made their way to Hong Kong, and then to the U.S. Other companies released different kinds of electronic pets in U.S. stores. The pet craze had hit the States!

So the next time you play with your electronic pet, remember — it all began in Japan!

It's not easy to find the perfect electronic pet for you. There are so many to choose from! Here is a list of some of the most popular electronic pets in the U.S.:

Tamagotchi™

TAMAGOTCHI is the "original virtual pet." It was invented in Japan. In the Japanese language, TAMAGOTCHI means "cute little egg" or "lovable egg."

Living inside the egg is a bird-creature. TAMAGOTCHI eats buns and snacks on candy. You can play a guessing game with TAMAGOTCHI. With this game, you have five chances to guess which way the TAMAGOTCHI bird will look — left or right. If three or more of your guesses are right, you win the game!

As TAMAGOTCHI grows older, it gets bigger and changes its appearance. If you take good care of it, it will grow into a cute, happy creature. But if you neglect it, it will grow into a scary, unhappy creature. Each time you hatch a new pet, you could end up with something different.

TAMAGOTCHI comes in different colors.

If you don't take good care of TAMAGOTCHI, or if it gets too old, it will return to its home planet.

Giga Pets™

This line of electronic pets was invented in the U.S. by Tiger Electronics. GIGA PETS change their appearance slightly as they grow. If you don't take good care of your pet, it will die and become an angel.

- Digital Doggie™:
  This pet walks and plays against a background of grass and sky. It eats dog food, snacks on bones, and plays fetch with a ball.

- Compu Kitty™: When this pet is a kitten, it drinks milk. When it becomes a cat, it eats solid food. It's always ready for a yummy fish snack. For fun, it chases butterflies.

- Baby T-Rex™: This tiny dino (from the movie *The Lost World*) starts out eating eggs, then moves on to meat bones when it gets older. Its favorite snack is pizza. A young T-Rex learns to play by chasing mice, then moves on to cars!

- Microchimp™: Living in a cyberspace jungle, this mischievous monkey loves bananas and coconuts best. This is one pet that likes to play with its food — it gets happy by juggling coconuts. This pet also has an extra feature. You can train it and teach it tricks!

- **Electronic Alien™**: This out-of-this-world pet lives in a black-and-yellow case. Its favorite Earth foods are eggs and candy. When it's playtime, it chases a UFO.

- **Bit Critter™**: When this computer creature isn't munching on batteries and computer chips, it's shooting computer bugs in cyberspace. You can also teach Bit Critter a trick or two.

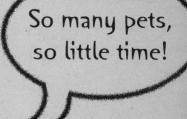

So many pets, so little time!

No matter what kind of electronic pet you have, the ways you take care of your pet are basically the same. By touching a button, you can call up different pictures on your pet's screen. Here is what the pictures will let you do:

1. **FEED YOUR PET.**
   You can either feed your pet a meal or a snack.

2. **TURN OUT THE LIGHTS.**
   Your pet will go to sleep on its own. GIGA PETS™ even take naps during the day. When your pet goes to sleep, you must turn out the lights or your pet will be unhappy. If you have a GIGA PET, you'll have to turn the lights on again when it wakes up.

3. **PLAY WITH YOUR PET.**
   You can play a different computer game with each pet.

4. **GO TO THE DOCTOR.**
   If your pet is sick, a picture will come on the screen to let you know. GIGA PETS visit a veterinarian in cyberspace. TAMAGOTCHI™ gets a shot when it isn't feeling well.

5. **CLEAN UP.**
   You can clean up after your pet when it goes to the

bathroom. If you have a GIGA PET, you can also give it a bath.

6. **CHECK YOUR SCORE.**
At any time, you can find out your pet's age and weight, and learn how happy, full, healthy, and well-behaved it is. (If you have a TAMAGOTCHI, a good score is a full discipline bar, and four full hearts for Hunger and Happiness. If you have a GIGA PET, try for a high score of 99 in Health, Discipline, Happiness, Hunger, and Overall score.)

7. **DISCIPLINE.**
If your pet is misbehaving, you can scold it.

8. **TRAIN IT.**
Some pets have an extra button that lets you teach it tricks.

Isn't it amazing what electronic pets can do? For special tips on how to use these functions, see Chapter Seven.

CHAPTER FOUR
Ten Reasons Why an Electronic Pet Is Better Than a Real Pet

You've just read about all the amazing things electronic pets can do. Still, I bet some of you out there are saying, "Big deal! Real pets can do that! And they're cuddly, too!"

Well, I still say electronic pets are better than real pets anyday. Just check out this list to find out what makes electronic pets the best:

1. Electronic pets don't make you sneeze.

2. Electronic pets don't shed all over your carpet.

3. You can't bring real pets to the movies, restaurants, the mall, or most other places — but you can take electronic pets almost anywhere!

4. Electronic pets won't chew up your favorite sweater.

5. Cleaning up after an electronic pet is a lot easier — and a lot less smelly!

6. Electronic pets don't chase cars or get lost.

7. Electronic pets don't get fleas (although they might get a computer bug or two!).

8. You don't have to take electronic pets for long walks in the rain or snow — unless you want to!

9. You can't hang real pets on your backpack.

10. Electronic pets don't bite!

Electronic pets are the best!

You've just brought home your first electronic pet. What do you do? Do you rip open the package and start pressing buttons?

No! If you want your electronic pet to live a long and happy life, it's best to take good care of it right from the beginning. To make sure your pet gets off on the right foot (or paw, or wing), check out these special cybertips:

1. BEFORE YOU DO ANYTHING, READ THE INSTRUCTIONS.

I know instructions don't look like a lot of fun. But by reading them carefully, you'll learn lots of important things about taking care of your pet.

Make sure to read through all of the instructions — don't just read the part about turning on your pet, and skip the rest. Sometimes there are things you have to do as soon as your pet is born. If you don't read the instructions, you won't know what to do.

If some parts of the instructions are a little confusing, ask someone in your family to help you figure them out. Sometimes two heads are better than one!

When you're done with the instructions, DON'T THROW THEM AWAY. You might forget how to feed, play with, or discipline your pet. Your instructions will also tell you how to change the battery when it wears out. If you can, keep your instructions someplace safe and handy, like a desk drawer.

2. PICK THE BEST TIME TO START YOUR PET.

As soon as your pet is born, it will need lots of attention. Pets usually beep more in the first two hours after they are born than during any other time in their lives.

So before you turn on your pet, make sure you will have nothing to do for a few hours. DON'T start your pet if:

- you have homework to do.
- you know your parents are taking you out somewhere.
- you have to go to school.
- you have to clean your room.
- you have to eat dinner soon.

If you start your pet during one of the above (or another "bad" time), the noise your pet makes will drive everyone around you crazy. And someone will probably say, "Turn that thing off!" Your pet won't like that one bit.

The best time to start your pet is when you have a few hours of free time ahead of you. Saturday morning is a good time. Then you'll have a whole weekend to play with your pet. Or you might try starting your pet after your homework is done, if you have some free time before bedtime.

If you can, you might want to start your pet at the beginning of a vacation from school. Then you'll have plenty of time to learn how to become an electronic pet expert!

3. DON'T FORGET TO SET THE TIME.

The first thing you will need to do when you start your pet is set the time. The instructions will tell you how to do this.

When you set the time, pay attention to the letters AM and PM. You probably know that AM is from midnight to 11:59 in the morning, and PM is from noon to 11:59 at night. Make sure that you set the time correctly. (It's okay if you are off by a minute or two.)

If you forget to set the time, or choose AM or PM by mistake, your pet will not go to sleep at the proper time. It may sleep all day, or keep you awake at night, and that's no fun. So set the time right from the start!

4. BE READY TO NAME YOUR PET.

If you have a GIGA PET™ you'll be able to give your pet a name up to ten letters long. You might want to plan ahead so that when the time comes to enter the letters on screen, you'll be ready.

Choosing the perfect name for a pet can be a real challenge. You could look through a baby book to find a name. Or maybe you could name your pet after:

* *your favorite book character.*
* *your favorite actor.*
* *your favorite singer.*
* *your favorite food.*
* *your favorite color.*

My pet's name
is Broccoli!

5. GIVE YOUR NEWBORN PET LOTS OF ATTENTION.

When your pet gets older, you may need to check it every half hour or so. But a newborn pet needs a lot more help.

As soon as your pet is born, check its Health meter. Find out how much food, happiness, and discipline it needs. Then get to work! Feed and play with your pet right away. Then check the meter again. You will probably need to feed and play with your pet every five minutes or so at first.

In the last chapter, I told you how important it is to read the instructions. Well, the instructions don't always tell you everything you need to know about taking care of your pet. Sometimes, you need a little extra help. That's where this chapter comes in.

Here is a list of problems you might be having with your pet. With luck, you'll find what you need, and you and your pet will be smiling in no time!

PROBLEM: My pet's alert signal is on and I can't get rid of it!

ANSWER:

If your pet's alert signal won't turn off, it could be one of two things:

1. Your pet is being naughty, or
2. Your pet needs something that you haven't done yet.

To find out what the problem is, check your pet's Health meter. If it seems to be happy, full, and healthy, then your pet probably needs to be disciplined. Scold it once and see if the alert signal goes away.

If disciplining doesn't help, then try the pictures on the screen one at a time until you find the problem. Try giving it a meal AND a snack (often a snack will do the trick). Play a few games with it. See if it needs to go to the doctor or get a shot. If you have a GIGA PET™ try giving it a bath, or try turning the lights out — it just might be trying to take a nap. Once you've tried everything, the alert signal should disappear.

PROBLEM: My pet doesn't go to sleep at night, and it sleeps all day.

ANSWER:

The pet's internal clock automatically tells it when to go to sleep at night. Depending on the kind of pet you have and how old it is, it should fall asleep anywhere between 8:00 and 10:00 at night.

If you pet doesn't fall asleep at these times, it means you've set the clock wrong. But don't worry. You can fix the time without disturbing your pet.

First, clear the screen.

If you have a TAMAGOTCHI™, press the B button until the clock appears. Press the A and C buttons at the same time. The word SET will appear on the screen. Press the A button to change the hour and the B button to change the minutes. Press C to enter the new time, and press B to see your pet again.

If you have a GIGA PET hit the MODE button until the clock appears. Hold down the ENTER button for about two seconds. When the numbers start to flash, you can change the time by pressing LEFT to change the hour and RIGHT to change the minutes. When you're done, hit ENTER to set the time.

PROBLEM: My electronic pet fell asleep with its alert signal on. Is there any way I can wake up my pet and give it what it needs?

ANSWER:

If you have a TAMAGOTCHI it will probably wake itself up at some point so you can take care of it. If have a GIGA PET you should be able to wake it up yourself and take care of the problem. Try turning the light on. If your pet won't wake up, discipline it. Turn the light on again. If you are lucky, your pet will wake up for a little while. After you're done playing with it, it will go back to sleep on its own.

PROBLEM: My electronic pet isn't making any noise.

ANSWER:

You may have turned off the sound by mistake. If you have a TAMAGOTCHI, try pressing the A and C buttons at the same time and see if the sound comes back on.

If you have a GIGA PET, hit the MODE button until the clock appears. There should be a little picture of a bell on the screen underneath the time. If not, press the RIGHT button and the bell should appear.

PROBLEM: I keep feeding my pet snacks, but it's still hungry.

ANSWER:

Snacks are good for keeping your pet happy — but not for filling its tummy. To keep your pet full, feed it meals, not snacks.

PROBLEM: A scary-looking picture popped up on the screen, and my pet's Health score is dropping. What should I do?

ANSWER:
Your pet is probably sick. Follow the instructions and take your pet to the vet. The scary picture should disappear right away, and its Health score will improve slowly.

PROBLEM: The instructions on my TAMAGOTCHI say I shouldn't let my pet get too fat. But I did. Can I help my pet lose weight?

ANSWER:
No problem! Just play with your pet a few times and its weight will go down. Even electronic pets need exercise!

PROBLEM: I keep playing games with my TAMAGOTCHI, but it won't get any happier.

ANSWER:
That's probably because you are losing the guessing game instead of winning. To win, you need to get at least three out of five guesses right. If you keep losing, don't give up. Keep playing. As soon as you win one game, your TAMAGOTCHI's Happiness will increase by one full heart.

PROBLEM: It's getting hard to see the pictures on my visual pet's screen.

ANSWER:

If the pictures are getting weaker, it means you will need a new battery soon. The instructions will tell you how an adult can change the batteries for you. Of course, this might mean that you will lose your electronic pet. But don't worry. You can always start again with a new one!

PROBLEM: CyberGirl, your answers aren't helping me at all! I did what you said, and my electronic pet is still in trouble.

ANSWER:

Sorry! Not every problem has an easy answer. If you've tried everything and nothing works, press the RESET button on the back of your pet and start over with a new pet. If you still have a problem with your new pet, write to the company that makes it. If you can't find the address in the instructions or on the box, ask for help at your local library.

Try, try again!

CHAPTER SEVEN
Tips for Raising a Healthy Pet

You're probably worried that your pet will become an angel soon or go back to its home planet. I know how you feel. CyberGirls have real feelings, too, you know.

That's why in this chapter, you'll find tips to help keep your pet around for a long time. In Japan, one TAMAGOTCHI™ lasted for thirty days. With enough care, GIGA PETS™ can last as long as the battery does — about one hundred days.

Who knows? Follow these tips, and maybe you'll break the record for the longest-lasting pet!

1. **When it's awake, check your pet every half hour if you can.**
This is the best way to make sure that your pet's Hunger and Happiness don't drop too low. The more attention you give your pet, the longer it will live.

2. **Learn how to discipline your pet properly.**
All pets need discipline once in awhile. GIGA PETS need more discipline than TAMAGOTCHI . Your instructions will tell you the best times to discipline your pet. But no matter what kind of pet you have, don't overdo it. Too much discipline will make your pet unhappy and unhealthy.

After you scold your pet, play a few games with it right

away — even if your pet deserved to be scolded. This will quickly bring your pet's Happiness back up again.

3. Discover the need to feed.

Remember, feeding your pet snacks won't make it full. Instead, feed your pet meals. If you have a TAMAGOTCHI, one meal equals one full heart. If you have a GIGA PET, one meal usually equals 20 points. (Use a little math to get the best Hunger score. If your pet has 71 Hunger points, feed it one meal. Your score should be somewhere in the 90s. But don't feed it two meals, or your pet will refuse to eat.)

After you play with your pet, check to see how hungry it is. Sometimes playing with a pet can make it hungry, and you'll need to feed it right away.

4. Bedtime tips:

Your pet will fall asleep at night by itself when it is tired. A newborn TAMAGOTCHI will fall asleep at 8 PM. As it gets older, it will fall asleep at 9 PM and then at 10 PM. A GIGA PET will fall asleep around 9:15 PM no matter how old it is.

It's a good idea to keep track of your pet's bedtime so you can take care of it before it goes to sleep. A few minutes before it sacks out, check to see how happy, hungry, and healthy it is and take care of it if you need to.

When your pet goes to sleep, it needs you to turn out the lights for it. If you don't, its Happiness will go down.

If you can't stay awake until your pet goes to sleep, ask someone in your family to turn out the lights for you.

5. Wake-Up tips:

Your pet will wake up on its own in the morning. A newborn TAMAGOTCHI sleeps until 9 AM and will sleep until 10 AM when it gets older. GIGA PETS are early risers. They wake up about 7 AM.

It's a good idea to check on your pet as soon as it wakes up. A GIGA PET goes to the bathroom right away, so be ready to clean up after it. It will also have a low score in the morning, so you'll have to spend some time feeding and playing with it.

Your TAMAGOTCHI's score will not go down as it sleeps. You'll probably have time to make yourself happy and full before you take care of this pet.

6. Naptime tips:

Your GIGA PET will take short naps during the day. That's another good reason to keep your pet with you at all times, if possible. Your pet will be happiest if you turn out the lights as soon as it goes to sleep.

My Electronic Pet Tips

The longer you take care of your electronic pet, the more you will learn about it. Use this space to write down tips you discover for keeping your pet healthy.

Cybersecrets

Birthday Surprise

Keeping your pet close by all the time will guarantee that you don't miss those special moments in its life. When a GIGA PET gets a year older, a birthday cake appears on the screen and the song "Happy Birthday" plays. When a TAMAGOTCHI is ready to grow and change its appearance, music plays and the pet does a little dance!

Fast Food

Your TAMAGOTCHI needs to eat more than one meal to be full, but you're in a hurry. What can you do? Instead of waiting until your pet finishes each meal, hit the B button. Your pet will be able to eat its next meal right away.

Freeze Frame

If you ignore your electronic pet, it will die or go back to its home planet. But some electronic pet owners have found a way to "freeze" their pets when they're too busy to take care of them. They go into the clock set mode and leave it there. When they leave the clock set mode, their pet is the same as it was before they left it. The score hasn't gone up or down. (Don't use this trick if you're in a contest to see how long your pet will live — that would be cheating!)

Sore Loser

If you're in the middle of playing a guessing game with Tamagotchi and you know you're going to lose, you can leave the game before it ends by pressing the c button.

So far, you love everything about your electronic pet. You love to feed it and play with it. You hug it every night before you go to sleep. There's only one problem:

Your electronic pet is not welcome in school.

No matter how much you beg, and plead, and cry, your teacher will not let you feed your pet during math class. She does not care if it goes to the bathroom right in the middle of a pop quiz.

Can you really blame her? After all, you wouldn't appreciate it if someone kept beeping at you when you were trying to teach the capital of Ohio. Your teacher has a point.

So what do you do? Don't despair. Just because you can't take care of your pet during class doesn't mean that it isn't long for this world. There are things you can do to keep your pet going during school days.

• FIND A BABY-SITTER.

Is there someone in your family who doesn't go to school who can take care of your pet for you? Then you won't have to worry about your pet at all while you're at school, and you can concentrate on learning the capital of Ohio. You can still play with your pet after school and on weekends.

I know someone who can watch it!

• TURN DOWN THE SOUND.

If you are allowed to bring your pet to school and play with it during lunch and recess, then you'll need to turn off the sound while you're in class. If you have a TAMAGOTCHI™, press the A and C buttons at the same time. If you have a GIGA PET™, clear the screen, and press the B button until the time appears. Press the LEFT button to make the little bell appear. The sound will be turned off.

Just before you turn the sound off, take good care of your pet. Make sure all of its hearts are full, or that its scores are as high as they can be. If your pet is happy and full before you turn the sound off, it will be okay if you have to leave it alone for a few hours.

At recess or lunch, turn the sound on again. If you have a TAMAGOTCHI, press the A and C buttons at the same time again. If you have a GIGA PET go back to the time and press the RIGHT button until the bell appears again.

Take care of your pet's needs right away. Pay lots of attention to it while you can. Make sure it is as full and happy as possible before you turn the sound off again.

When school is out, give your pet lots of attention again. If you keep up this routine, your pet will probably last through the school week.

* Check Chapter Seven for the "freeze frame" tip, but be forewarned: This trick might not always work!

• RESET THE TIME.

While you're in school, you can "trick" your pet into thinking it's nighttime. Here's how:

1. As soon as you get to school, reset the clock to your pet's normal bedtime. Your pet will now go to sleep!
2. After school, reset the time to your pet's normal wake-up time. Now your pet will wake up!
3. Finally, reset the clock to the correct time, and continue caring for your pet.

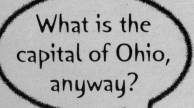

Playing with your electronic pet can be fun, but showing it off can be fun, too. Here are some ways to flaunt your pet with flair.

• HANG IT FROM A BACKPACK.

Keychain collectors already know the best way to accessorize their backpacks. But if you leave your backpack at home, don't forget to take your pet with you!

• WEAR IT AROUND YOUR NECK.

Kids in Japan love to hang their electronic pets from strings or chains and wear them around their necks. It's one way to make sure your pet will always be with you. Just make sure the chain isn't too delicate — your pet is heavy, and the chain may break. A silk cord works great, and so does a chain made of silver balls.

• DANGLE IT FROM A BELT LOOP.

Tuck in your shirt, hook on your pet, and you're ready to go. Just make sure you don't put your pet in the washing machine!

• HOOK IT TO YOUR OVERALLS.

If you prefer overalls to jeans, then this is the fashion statement for you. The key ring should easily attach to the fasteners on your overall straps. Besides, this is a great way to keep your pet close to your heart.

• KEEP IT IN YOUR RING BINDER.

Attach it to a ring in your binder, and you'll have a handy way to keep your pet nearby on school days. This method does not work great if you're playing basketball or going to the movies.

• MAKE IT A POCKET PET.

Snuggled in your pocket, your pet will be safe from harm. It's not the best way to make a fashion statement, however, so if you want to show off your pet's color or style, this is not the look for you.

I hooked mine to a buttonhole on my favorite jacket!

Taking care of your electronic pet can be more fun if you can share the experience with friends. Why not form a club? Follow these steps to make yours the coolest club outside of cyberspace.

1. Recruit members.

Find friends who want to join your club. Have each member write his or her name on the Club Membership List on page 37.

2. Dare to share.

Each member of your club doesn't have to have his or her own pet. Sharing can be fun, too. After all, taking care of an electronic pet can be hard work. You could try giving a friend your pet to take care of on odd-numbered days, while you take care of it on even-numbered days.

Your whole club could even share one pet. Each member could take care of the pet for one or more days a week. Make a schedule that shows who is on pet duty each day so that there are no misunderstandings.

Can we join your club?

3. Decide when you'll meet.

Many clubs meet once a week, but since electronic pets need so much care, you might want to meet more often than that. Your meetings don't have to be long. You might just meet for a few minutes each day to talk about how your pets are doing.

4. Name your club.

A good club will have a catchy name. How about the Pet Pros? Or the Cyberclub? See how many names you can come up with, then take a vote.

5. Form a phone chain.

Something's wrong with your pet and you don't know what to do? Call up one of your club members. He or she might know a trick or two to help get your pet on its feet. Or you might be able to help a club member who has a problem of her own.

6. Surf the Net.

If you are connected to the Internet, and you have your parents' permission, your club could surf the Net to find more information on your electronic pets. You may find news from the companies that make the pets, and tips from electronic pet experts. You might even be able to chat with electronic pet owners around the world. When you're searching for Web sites about electronic pets, good key words to try are "TAMAGOTCHI™," "GIGA PET™," and "virtual pets."

7. Start a newsletter.

Use a computer or handwrite a club newsletter. You could write about new members in your club, new pets your club members have, club activities, and you could also list records made by club members. Photocopy your newsletter and give one to each club member.

8. Have a party.

See Chapter Eleven of this book for party ideas.

9. Have pet contests.

See Chapter Twelve of this book to find ways to compete with your pet.

I hope you can come to my party!

Club Membership List

Name	Phone Number	Pet's Name

CHAPTER ELEVEN
Throw a Pet Party

In my world, we love to have parties with our electronic pets. Why not invite your friends to a special pet party? You don't have to go to a lot of trouble. Besides, you need to have a little fun after taking such good care of your pet!

Here are some ways to make your party one to remember:

1. SEND INVITATIONS.

Make your own invitations out of construction paper or on your computer. Be sure to include the time your party will start, and the address where it will be held. Don't forget to remind everyone to bring their electronic pets.

2. DECORATE.

These decorations will make any electronic pet lover smile:

- Cut out pet shapes, tie a string to the top of each one, and hang them from the ceiling.
- Blow up balloons. Don't they look like eggs? Use a dark marker to draw electronic bird-creatures on the balloons.
- Serve snacks in plastic pet food dishes (clean, of course).
- For party favors, hide candy or other treats in small plastic eggs (you can find these in most stores in March and April).

3. HAVE A BIRTHDAY PARTY.

If you are about to start a new pet, give the party a birthday theme to welcome your new pet to the world. Better yet, invite a bunch of friends ready to start new pets, and start all of your pets at exactly the same time.

At the party, serve birthday cake. You can even sing this special song to the tune of "Happy Birthday" (we sing it on every pet's birthday on my world):

> Happy Birthday dear pet.
> Let's go to the vet.
> Then I'll give you a bath.
> And you'll get all wet!

4. CHOW DOWN.

Just because this is an electronic pet party doesn't mean you can serve electronic food. Serve any or all of these real foods in honor of your electronic pets:

SNACKS

- Put out fish-shaped crackers in bowls for people with electronic cats.
- Serve potato chips and tell people they are edible micro chips.
- Put out bowls of bite-sized candy in honor of those electronic pets with sweet tooths.

MAIN DISHES

• JURASSIC PIZZAS

Follow these steps to make a lip-smacking lunch for people with electronic dinosaurs. Get an adult to help you.

1. Use one English muffin or bagel for each party guest. Separate each muffin or bagel into two halves and lay them on a cookie sheet.
2. Spoon tomato sauce (sauce from a jar is fine) on each muffin or bagel half.
3. Slice green olives (to make dinosaur scales) and sprinkle them on the tomato sauce.
4. Sprinkle shredded mozzarella cheese on top of each pizza.
5. Put the cookie sheet in a pre-heated 400-degree oven and cook until the cheese melts.

• BONE BREAD

People with electronic dogs will dig this dish. Get an adult to help you.

1. Open a package of refrigerated dinner rolls — the kind that come in a round tube.
2. Separate the rolls. Arrange seven of the rolls on a cookie sheet in a bone shape:

3. If you're serving the bread with pizza, sprinkle the top with grated Parmesan cheese.
4. Bake the rolls according to the directions on the package. Let them cool off a little before you dig in!

DESSERT

• BANANA–COCONUT SUNDAES

People with electronic monkeys will flip for this tasty tropical treat.

1. Put one scoop of vanilla ice cream in each guest's bowl.
2. Slice up several bananas and arrange them around the ice cream.
3. Pour chocolate sauce on top.
4. Sprinkle with shredded coconut (you can find this in bags at your grocery store).

5. PLAY GAMES.

Check out Chapter Twelve of this book for games you can play with your electronic pets. You and your human guests can play your own games, too. Try these twists on traditional party favorites:

- Instead of "Pin the Tail on the Donkey," play "Pin the Tail on the Doggie." Just draw an electronic dog on a large piece of construction paper, make a paper tail, and you're ready to go.

- Play "Hot Potato" with a hard-boiled egg.

- Play "Telephone" using one of these hard-to-remember messages:

Sally went to cyberspace to sip spicy apple cider.

My electronic pet woke up, ate a meal, played a game, ate a snack, took a bath, went to the vet, and went to sleep.

Victor thought his electronic pet was very electronic and electronically vivacious.

During the summer, you'll have lots of free time to play with your pet. Why not make a game out of it? In fact, why not hold a series of games?

Some events might take only a few minutes. Others could last all summer long. Use the record sheet on page 46 to keep track of the medal winners.

Are you ready to play? On your mark, get set, go!

• The Long–Distance Race

Hold ☞contest to see which player can keep a pet alive the longest. To make the contest fair, all players should start a new pet at exactly the same time. Gather all the players together. Everyone should start their pets at the count of "three."

See how many players can make their pets last all summer — or even longer!

• The Five–Round Relay

For this contest, you'll need players with the same kind of electronic pet.

TAMAGOTCHI™ owners should each play five rounds of the guessing game. The player who wins the most games out of the five wins the contest. If it's a tie, have the players play one more guessing game. Whoever gets the most guesses right in one game is the winner.

DIGITAL DOGGIE™ owners could play five rounds of fetch and add up the number of seconds left on the screen each time. The player with the highest number is the winner.

See what other kinds of contests you can make up based on the game functions of other electronic pets.

• The Fifteen-Minute Fling

This contest works best with GIGA PETS™. Set a timer for fifteen minutes. When the timer starts, all players should try to bring up their pet's score. When the timer goes off, the player with the highest overall score is the winner.

For a variation of this game, set the timer for five minutes, ten minutes, or even an hour.

• The Multi-Pet Juggle

Some contestants in your games may have many different kinds of pets. If you think keeping one pet alive is tricky, try keeping two, three, or even more pets alive at the same time! For this contest, see who can keep the most pets alive at once for the longest amount of time. As soon as one pet's life is over, that player is out of the contest.

What other events for your electronic pet can you think of? Describe them here:

_____

_____

_____

_____

_____

_____

_____

_____

_____

_____

_____

_____

_____

_____

_____

_____

_____

_____

_____

_____

_____

_____

Medal Winners

1. The Long–Distance Race

Gold Medal _____ Days Pet Kept Alive _____
Silver Medal _____ Days Pet Kept Alive _____
Bronze Medal _____ Days Pet Kept Alive _____

2. The Five–Round Relay

Gold Medal _____ Score _____
Silver Medal _____ Score _____
Bronze Medal _____ Score _____

3. The Fifteen–Minute Fling

Gold Medal _____ Score _____
Silver Medal _____ Score _____
Bronze Medal _____ Score _____

4. The Multi–Pet Juggle

Gold Medal _____ * of Pets ____ Days Lasted ____
Silver Medal _____ * of Pets ____ Days Lasted ____
Bronze Medal _____ * of Pets ____ Days Lasted ____

OTHER WINNERS

_____

_____

_____

_____

_____

_____

_____

_____

_____

_____

_____

_____

_____

_____

_____

_____

_____

_____

_____

_____

_____

_____

_____

_____

CHAPTER THIRTEEN
Are You a Pet Head?

I know the symptoms. I've seen them before. It happens when people get too involved with their electronic pets. They walk around in a daze. Their eyes get a weird glazed look. It's not a pretty sight. In my world, we call these people Pet Heads.

Don't let this happen to you! Electronic pets are fun, but so are other things in life. Take this quiz to see if you have become a Pet Head:

1. Do you ask your mom to make you microchip cookies?

2. When your alarm clock beeps, do you try to feed it a snack?

3. When you go to sleep, do you count electronic sheep?

4. Have you thought about getting your nose pierced so you can hang your pet from it?

5. Have your friends started beeping at you because they know it's the only way to get your attention?

6. Have you been wondering what it would be like to have electronic parents?

7. Instead of watching TV at night, do you stare at your electronic pet's screen for hours?

8. Are you starting to build muscle in your button-pressing finger?

9. Is your real pet jealous of your electronic pet?

10. Do you cuddle your electronic pet at night instead of your teddy bear?

SCORE

- If you answered yes to three questions or less, there is still hope for you. You've got a good head on your shoulders. But take this test every week just to make sure.

- If you answered yes to four to six questions, be careful! You are in danger of becoming a serious Pet Head. Turn the sound off for awhile and read a good book.

- If you answered yes to seven to nine questions, you are a certified Pet Head. If you had a RESET button, it would be time to reset you! Give your pet to someone else to take care of while you recover. (Just make sure they don't become a Pet Head, too!)

- If you answered yes to all ten questions, you are a Super Pet Head. Take a nice long vacation somewhere far, far away from toy stores.

Cybersafety

On the serious side, don't let your electronic pet distract you too much, especially when you're doing something like crossing the street or riding your bicycle.

Nothing bad will happen to your pet if you wait a few minutes to answer its beep!

CHAPTER FOURTEEN
Lights Out!

Whether you're a Pet Head or not, you don't have to feel silly about showering your electronic pet with love. After all, that's what pets are for.

I keep my electronic pet in a special little box next to my bed. I put an old sock in the box so my pet is nice and cozy. Just before it falls asleep, I tell it a little bedtime story.

Telling the same story night after night can get a little boring. Use this handy story guide to make up your own story. Use a pencil to circle the letter next to the answer you want. The next night, erase your pencil marks and get ready to tell a whole new story.

Once upon a time, there lived an
    a. electronic bird.
    b. electronic dog.
    c. electronic cat.
    d. electronic monkey.
    e. electronic dinosaur.
    f. electronic alien.
    g. electronic computer-creature.

The little pet was zipping through cyberspace one day when it came across
    a. a deep, dark jungle.
    b. a deserted spaceship.

    c. an underground cave.

    d. an enchanted castle.

The pet nervously crawled inside. Much to its surprise, it saw

    a. a ferocious lion.

    b. an eight-headed alien.

    c. a giant spider.

    d. a fire-breathing dragon.

"Don't hurt me!" cried the pet. But the creature looked sad. "Don't worry," it said. "I'm just looking for my lost

    a. baseball card collection."

    b. pair of lucky underwear."

    c. jelly beans."

    d. giant rubber-band ball."

The pet smiled. "You're in luck," it said. "I just happen to have what you're looking for in my

    a. nostrils."

    b. sock drawer."

    c. secret hiding place."

    d. kitchen sink."

And they all lived happily ever after.

If you're like me, you'll want to remember everything about your pet. Use these pages to keep a diary of up to three different pets. Look back through your diary once in awhile to see if you can learn anything about how to take better care of your next pet.

Here's how I filled in a page of my pet's diary:

DAY 12

Draw pet here

Wake-up time: **7:05**

Bedtime: **9:13**

Today, my pet looked like:

Feeding Times:
7:06
9:00
11:00
12:30

How Many Meals?
3
1
2
1

Cleaning Times:
7:05
3:15

Vet Trips:

Time Games Played:
7:07
9:01

Scores:
10 seconds
12 seconds

Final score of the day:
99 Health
91 Hunger
6 Age
75 Happiness
23 Discipline
1 lb Weight
81 Total Score

87

KIND OF PET: Compu Kitty

NAME: BaBY 2

DAY MY PET WAS BORN: 1-5-P8

TIME MY PET WAS BORN: 7.00 9m

DAY MY PET LEFT EARTH: _____

TIME MY PET LEFT EARTH: _____

DAY 1

Wake-up time: 7:00 am

Bedtime: 10:00 PM

Today, my pet looked like:

Draw pet here

Feeding Times:

8:00 am

7:00 PM

How Many Meals?

Cleaning Times:

7:05 PM

Vet Trips:

1 a week

Time Games Played:

Scores:

Final score of the day: _____ Health   _____ Happiness
_____ Hunger   _____ Discipline
_____ Age   _____ Weight
_____ Total Score

DAY 2

Wake-up time: _____

Bedtime: _____

Today, my pet looked like: ➤

Draw pet here

Feeding Times:
_____
_____
_____
_____

How Many Meals?
_____
_____
_____
_____

Cleaning Times:
_____
_____
_____

Vet Trips:
_____
_____

_____
_____

Time Games Played:
_____
_____
_____
_____

Scores:
_____
_____
_____
_____

Final score of the day:

_____Health   _____Happiness
_____Hunger   _____Discipline
_____Age   _____Weight
                  _____Total Score

DAY 3

Wake-up time: _____

Bedtime: _____

Today, my pet looked like: →

Draw pet here

Feeding Times:
_____
_____
_____
_____
_____

How Many Meals?
_____
_____
_____
_____
_____

Cleaning Times:
_____
_____
_____

_____
_____
_____

Vet Trips:
_____
_____

_____
_____

Time Games Played:
_____
_____
_____
_____

Scores:
_____
_____
_____
_____

Final score of the day:

_____Health   _____Happiness
_____Hunger   _____Discipline
_____Age   _____Weight
                  _____Total Score

DAY 4

Wake-up time: _____

Bedtime: _____

Today, my pet looked like: ➚

Draw pet here

Feeding Times:
_____
_____
_____
_____
_____

How Many Meals?
_____
_____
_____
_____
_____

Cleaning Times:
_____
_____
_____

_____
_____
_____

Vet Trips:
_____
_____

_____
_____

Time Games Played:
_____
_____
_____
_____

Scores:
_____
_____
_____
_____

Final score of the day: _____Health   _____Happiness
                            _____Hunger   _____Discipline
                            _____Age   _____Weight
                                                  _____Total Score

DAY 5

Wake-up time: _____

Bedtime: _____

Today, my pet looked like: ←

Draw pet here

Feeding Times:

_____
_____
_____
_____
_____

How Many Meals?

_____
_____
_____
_____
_____

Cleaning Times:

_____
_____
_____

Vet Trips:

_____
_____

Time Games Played:

_____
_____
_____
_____

Scores:

_____
_____
_____
_____

Final score of the day:

_____Health _____Happiness
_____Hunger _____Discipline
_____Age   _____Weight
             _____Total Score

DAY 6

Wake-up time: _____

Bedtime: _____

Today, my pet looked like: ⟶

Draw pet here

Feeding Times:
_____
_____
_____
_____
_____

How Many Meals?
_____
_____
_____
_____
_____

Cleaning Times:
_____
_____
_____

Vet Trips:
_____
_____

Time Games Played:
_____
_____
_____
_____

Scores:
_____
_____
_____
_____

Final score of the day:

_____Health   _____Happiness
_____Hunger   _____Discipline
_____Age   _____Weight
                 _____Total Score

DAY 7

Wake-up time: _____

Bedtime: _____

Today, my pet looked like: →

Draw pet here

Feeding Times:
_____
_____
_____
_____
_____

How Many Meals?
_____
_____
_____
_____

Cleaning Times:
_____
_____
_____

_____
_____

Vet Trips:
_____
_____

_____
_____

Time Games Played:
_____
_____
_____
_____

Scores:
_____
_____
_____
_____

Final score of the day:

_____Health   _____Happiness
_____Hunger   _____Discipline
_____Age   _____Weight
                     _____Total Score

DAY 8

Wake-up time: _____

Bedtime: _____

Today, my pet looked like: ➜

Draw pet here

Feeding Times:
_____
_____
_____
_____
_____

How Many Meals?
_____
_____
_____
_____
_____

Cleaning Times:
_____
_____
_____

_____
_____
_____

Vet Trips:
_____
_____

_____
_____

Time Games Played:
_____
_____
_____
_____

Scores:
_____
_____
_____
_____

Final score of the day: _____Health   _____Happiness
                             _____Hunger   _____Discipline
                             _____Age   _____Weight
                                                 _____Total Score

DAY 9

Wake-up time: _____

Bedtime: _____

Today, my pet looked like:

Draw pet here

Feeding Times:
_____
_____
_____
_____
_____

How Many Meals?
_____
_____
_____
_____
_____

Cleaning Times:
_____
_____
_____

_____
_____
_____

Vet Trips:
_____
_____

_____
_____

Time Games Played:
_____
_____
_____
_____

Scores:
_____
_____
_____
_____

Final score of the day: _____Health   _____Happiness
                            _____Hunger   _____Discipline
                            _____Age   _____Weight
                                               _____Total Score

DAY 10

Wake-up time: _____

Bedtime: _____

Today, my pet looked like: ⟍

Draw pet here

Feeding Times:
_____
_____
_____
_____

How Many Meals?
_____
_____
_____
_____
_____

Cleaning Times:
_____
_____
_____

_____
_____

Vet Trips:
_____
_____

_____
_____

Time Games Played:
_____
_____
_____
_____

Scores:
_____
_____
_____
_____

Final score of the day: _____Health   _____Happiness
                           _____Hunger   _____Discipline
                           _____Age   _____Weight
                                           _____Total Score

DAY 11

Wake-up time: _____

Bedtime: _____

Today, my pet looked like: ↗

Draw pet here

Feeding Times:
_____
_____
_____
_____
_____

How Many Meals?
_____
_____
_____
_____
_____

Cleaning Times:
_____
_____
_____

_____
_____

Vet Trips:
_____
_____

_____
_____

Time Games Played:
_____
_____
_____
_____

Scores:
_____
_____
_____
_____

Final score of the day:

_____Health   _____Happiness
_____Hunger   _____Discipline
_____Age   _____Weight
                 _____Total Score

DAY 12

Wake-up time: _____

Bedtime: _____

Today, my pet looked like:

Draw pet here

Feeding Times:
_____
_____
_____
_____
_____

How Many Meals?
_____
_____
_____
_____

Cleaning Times:
_____
_____
_____

_____
_____
_____

Vet Trips:
_____
_____

_____
_____

Time Games Played:
_____
_____
_____
_____

Scores:
_____
_____
_____
_____

Final score of the day: _____Health   _____Happiness
                           _____Hunger   _____Discipline
                           _____Age   _____Weight
                                             _____Total Score

DAY 13

Wake-up time: _____

Bedtime: _____

Today, my pet looked like: → [Draw pet here]

Feeding Times:
_____
_____
_____
_____
_____

How Many Meals?
_____
_____
_____
_____
_____

Cleaning Times:
_____
_____
_____

_____
_____
_____

Vet Trips:
_____
_____

_____
_____

Time Games Played:
_____
_____
_____
_____

Scores:
_____
_____
_____
_____

Final score of the day: _____Health   _____Happiness
                            _____Hunger   _____Discipline
                            _____Age   _____Weight
                                               _____Total Score

DAY 14

Wake-up time: _____

Bedtime: _____

Today, my pet looked like: ↗

Draw pet here

Feeding Times:
_____
_____
_____
_____
_____

How Many Meals?
_____
_____
_____
_____
_____

Cleaning Times:
_____
_____
_____

_____
_____
_____

Vet Trips:
_____
_____

_____
_____

Time Games Played:
_____
_____
_____
_____

Scores:
_____
_____
_____
_____

Final score of the day:

_____Health   _____Happiness
_____Hunger   _____Discipline
_____Age   _____Weight
              _____Total Score

EXTRA DAYS/NOTES

EXTRA DAYS/NOTES

EXTRA DAYS/NOTES

EXTRA DAYS/NOTES

EXTRA DAYS/NOTES

EXTRA DAYS/NOTES

PET 2

KIND OF PET: _____

NAME: _____

DAY MY PET WAS BORN: _____

TIME MY PET WAS BORN: _____

DAY MY PET LEFT EARTH: _____

TIME MY PET LEFT EARTH: _____

DAY 1

Wake-up time:_____

Bedtime: _____

Today, my pet looked like:

Draw pet here

Feeding Times:
_____
_____
_____
_____
_____

How Many Meals?
_____
_____
_____
_____
_____

Cleaning Times:
_____
_____
_____

_____
_____
_____

Vet Trips:
_____
_____

_____
_____

Time Games Played:
_____
_____
_____
_____

Scores:
_____
_____
_____
_____

Final score of the day: _____Health   _____Happiness
                           _____Hunger   _____Discipline
                           _____Age   _____Weight
                                              _____Total Score

DAY 2

Wake-up time:_____

Bedtime: _____

Today, my pet looked like: ⟶

Draw pet here

Feeding Times:
_____
_____
_____
_____
_____

How Many Meals?
_____
_____
_____
_____
_____

Cleaning Times:
_____
_____
_____

Vet Trips:
_____
_____

_____
_____
_____
_____

Time Games Played:
_____
_____
_____
_____

Scores:
_____
_____
_____
_____

Final score of the day: _____Health   _____Happiness
                             _____Hunger   _____Discipline
                             _____Age   _____Weight
                                               _____Total Score

DAY 3

Wake-up time: _____

Bedtime: _____

Today, my pet looked like: ←

Draw pet here

Feeding Times:

_____
_____
_____
_____
_____

Cleaning Times:

_____
_____
_____

Vet Trips:

_____
_____

Time Games Played:

_____
_____
_____
_____

How Many Meals?

_____
_____
_____
_____
_____

_____
_____
_____
_____

_____
_____

Scores:

_____
_____
_____
_____

Final score of the day: _____Health   _____Happiness
                            _____Hunger   _____Discipline
                            _____Age   _____Weight
                                                _____Total Score

DAY 4

Wake-up time: _____

Bedtime: _____

Today, my pet looked like: ➤

Draw pet here

Feeding Times:
_____
_____
_____
_____
_____

How Many Meals?
_____
_____
_____
_____
_____

Cleaning Times:
_____
_____
_____

_____
_____
_____

Vet Trips:
_____
_____

_____
_____

Time Games Played:
_____
_____
_____
_____

Scores:
_____
_____
_____

Final score of the day: _____Health   _____Happiness
                            _____Hunger   _____Discipline
                            _____Age   _____Weight
                                                _____Total Score

DAY 5

Wake-up time: _____

Bedtime: _____

Today, my pet looked like: ⟶

Draw pet here

Feeding Times:

_____
_____
_____
_____
_____

How Many Meals?

_____
_____
_____
_____
_____

Cleaning Times:

_____
_____
_____

_____
_____
_____

Vet Trips:

_____
_____

_____
_____

Time Games Played:

_____
_____
_____

Scores:

_____
_____
_____

Final score of the day: _____Health   _____Happiness
                            _____Hunger   _____Discipline
                            _____Age   _____Weight
                                                   _____Total Score

DAY 6

Wake-up time:_____

Bedtime: _____

Today, my pet looked like:

Draw pet here

Feeding Times:

_____
_____
_____
_____
_____

How Many Meals?

_____
_____
_____
_____
_____

Cleaning Times:

_____
_____
_____

_____
_____
_____

Vet Trips:

_____
_____

_____
_____

Time Games Played:

_____
_____
_____
_____

Scores:

_____
_____
_____
_____

Final score of the day: _____Health   _____Happiness
                            _____Hunger   _____Discipline
                            _____Age   _____Weight
                                              _____Total Score

DAY 7

Wake-up time: _____

Bedtime: _____

Today, my pet looked like: ➤

Draw pet here

Feeding Times:

_____
_____
_____
_____
_____

How Many Meals?

_____
_____
_____
_____
_____

Cleaning Times:

_____
_____
_____

_____
_____
_____

Vet Trips:

_____
_____

_____
_____

Time Games Played:

_____
_____
_____
_____

Scores:

_____
_____
_____
_____

Final score of the day: _____Health   _____Happiness
                         _____Hunger   _____Discipline
                         _____Age   _____Weight
                                            _____Total Score

DAY 8

Wake-up time: _____

Bedtime: _____

Today, my pet looked like: ⟍

Draw pet here

Feeding Times:
_____
_____
_____
_____
_____

How Many Meals?
_____
_____
_____
_____
_____

Cleaning Times:
_____
_____
_____

_____
_____
_____

Vet Trips:
_____
_____

_____
_____

Time Games Played:
_____
_____
_____
_____

Scores:
_____
_____
_____
_____

Final score of the day: _____Health   _____Happiness
                          _____Hunger   _____Discipline
                          _____Age   _____Weight
                                          _____Total Score

DAY 9

Wake-up time: _____

Bedtime: _____

Today, my pet looked like:

Draw pet here

Feeding Times:
_____
_____
_____
_____
_____

How Many Meals?
_____
_____
_____
_____
_____

Cleaning Times:
_____
_____
_____

_____
_____
_____

Vet Trips:
_____
_____

_____
_____

Time Games Played:
_____
_____
_____
_____

Scores:
_____
_____
_____
_____

Final score of the day: _____Health   _____Happiness
                           _____Hunger   _____Discipline
                           _____Age   _____Weight
                                                _____Total Score

DAY 10

Wake-up time:_____

Bedtime: _____

Today, my pet looked like: ⟍

Draw pet here

Feeding Times:
_____
_____
_____
_____
_____

How Many Meals?
_____
_____
_____
_____
_____

Cleaning Times:
_____
_____
_____

_____
_____
_____

Vet Trips:
_____
_____

_____
_____

Time Games Played:
_____
_____
_____
_____

Scores:
_____
_____
_____
_____

Final score of the day: _____Health   _____Happiness
                              _____Hunger   _____Discipline
                              _____Age   _____Weight
                                                _____Total Score

DAY 11

Wake-up time: _____

Bedtime: _____

Today, my pet looked like: →

Draw pet here

Feeding Times:
_____
_____
_____
_____
_____

Cleaning Times:
_____
_____
_____

Vet Trips:
_____
_____

Time Games Played:
_____
_____
_____
_____

How Many Meals?
_____
_____
_____
_____
_____
_____
_____
_____

Scores:
_____
_____
_____
_____

Final score of the day: _____Health   _____Happiness
                         _____Hunger   _____Discipline
                         _____Age   _____Weight
                                            _____Total Score

DAY 12

Wake-up time: _____

Bedtime: _____

Today, my pet looked like: →

Draw pet here

Feeding Times:
_____
_____
_____
_____
_____

How Many Meals?
_____
_____
_____
_____
_____

Cleaning Times:
_____
_____
_____

_____
_____
_____

Vet Trips:
_____
_____

_____
_____

Time Games Played:
_____
_____
_____
_____

Scores:
_____
_____
_____
_____

Final score of the day:

_____Health _____Happiness
_____Hunger _____Discipline
_____Age   _____Weight
               _____Total Score

DAY 13

Wake-up time: _____

Bedtime: _____

Today, my pet looked like: ➔

| Draw pet here |

Feeding Times:
_____
_____
_____
_____
_____

How Many Meals?
_____
_____
_____
_____
_____

Cleaning Times:
_____
_____
_____

_____
_____

Vet Trips:
_____
_____

_____

Time Games Played:
_____
_____
_____
_____

Scores:
_____
_____
_____
_____

Final score of the day:

_____Health   _____Happiness
_____Hunger   _____Discipline
_____Age   _____Weight
                _____Total Score

DAY 14

Wake-up time: _____

Bedtime: _____

Today, my pet looked like: ⟋

Draw pet here

Feeding Times: How Many Meals?
_____   _____
_____   _____
_____   _____
_____   _____
_____   _____

Cleaning Times:
_____   _____
_____   _____
_____   _____

Vet Trips:
_____   _____
_____   _____

Time Games Played: Scores:
_____   _____
_____   _____
_____   _____
_____   _____

Final score of the day: _____Health   _____Happiness
                            _____Hunger   _____Discipline
                            _____Age   _____Weight
                                             _____Total Score

EXTRA DAYS/NOTES

_____

_____

_____

_____

_____

_____

_____

_____

_____

_____

_____

_____

_____

_____

_____

_____

_____

_____

_____

_____

_____

_____

_____

EXTRA DAYS/NOTES

EXTRA DAYS/NOTES

EXTRA DAYS/NOTES

EXTRA DAYS/NOTES

_____

_____

_____

_____

_____

_____

_____

_____

_____

_____

_____

_____

_____

_____

_____

_____

_____

_____

_____

_____

_____

_____

_____

_____

All My Pets

No matter how well you take care of your electronic pet, it will leave you someday. Don't worry! You can always start more. Use this page to keep track of all the pets you take care of.

Pet's Name	Lived From
_____	_____
_____	_____
_____	_____
_____	_____
_____	_____
_____	_____
_____	_____
_____	_____
_____	_____
_____	_____
_____	_____
_____	_____
_____	_____
_____	_____
_____	_____
_____	_____

Collector's Checklist

One of the reasons electronic pets are so popular is because there are many styles and colors to collect. Use this list to keep track of the pets in your collections. Use the blank lines to add in new styles and models as they are introduced.

❑ Transparent turquoise Tamagotchi™

❑ Yellow Tamagotchi™ with orange details

❑ Red Tamagotchi™ with yellow details

❑ Purple Tamagotchi™ with pink details

❑ Green Tamagotchi™ with yellow details

❑ White Tamagotchi™ with blue details

❑ Digital Doggie™

❑ Compu Kitty™

❑ Baby T-Rex™

❑ Microchimp™

❑ Electronic Alien™

❑ Bit Critter™

❑ _____

❑ _____

❑ _____

❑ _____

❑ _____